To Dominique and Nicky

Also by David McKee:
Elmer
Elmer and Rose
Elmer and the Hippos
Elmer's Special Day

American edition published in 2011 by Andersen Press USA, an imprint of Andersen Press Ltd.
www.andersenpressusa.com

First published in Great Britain in 2007 by Andersen Press Ltd.,
20 Vauxhall Bridge Road, London SW1V 2SA.
Paperback edition first published in 2009 by Andersen Press Ltd.
Published in Australia by Random House Australia Pty.,
Level 3, 100 Pacific Highway, North Sydney, NSW 2060.

Distributed in the United States and Canada by
Lerner Publishing Group, Inc.
241 First Avenue North
Minneapolis, MN 55401 U.S.A.
www.lernerbooks.com

Library of Congress Cataloging-in-Publication Data Available.
ISBN: 978-0-7613-7410-7

Manufactured in Singapore by Tien Wah Press.
1 – TWP – 9/8/10
This book has been printed on acid-free paper.

David McKee
ELMER
and the Rainbow

Andersen Press USA

Elmer, the patchwork elephant, was in a cave, sheltering from a storm. With him were other elephants and birds. "Thunder and lightning are exciting," said Elmer. "And after the storm, we might see a rainbow."

When the storm had stopped,
Elmer and the birds went outside.
Elmer felt drops on his head.
"Oh," he said. "It's still raining!"
"Perhaps it's the rainbow crying,"
said a bird. "It's come out too soon
and lost its colors. Look!"

In the sky was a pale shape. "A rainbow without colors!" said Elmer. "That's awful. We must do something. I'll give it my colors."
"To do that, you'll have to find where it touches the ground," said a bird. "Nobody knows where that is."
"Well, what are we waiting for?" said Elmer. "Let's start searching. You go that way, and I'll go this."

"What are you looking for, Elmer?" called Lion.
"The end of the rainbow," said Elmer. "Have you seen it?"
"Which end?" asked Lion.
"Either end," said Elmer. "The rainbow's lost its colors. I can give it mine, if we can find the end."
"A rainbow without colors? That is serious," said Tiger. "Come on, Lion, we'd better search. You too, rabbits."
"We'll roar, when we find it," said Lion.

A little later, Elmer met Giraffe. "Elmer," she said, "there's something strange in the sky." "That's the rainbow," said Elmer, and he told her about the lost colors. "Can you see where it touches the ground?" Giraffe stretched very high. "No, I can't," she said. "What will happen to you, Elmer, if you give it your colors?" she asked. But Elmer was already on his way to get the elephants.

The elephants were still in the cave. "We're not coming out with that thing in the sky," they said. But when Elmer explained the problem, the elephants were keen to help.
"What about Elmer? What happens if he gives away his colors?" asked an elephant.
"I suppose he'll be like us," said his friend.
"Better that than a colorless rainbow!"

Elmer was with the monkeys when the
birds returned. "No luck so far," they said.
"We'll keep looking."
"Nobody can find the end of the rainbow,"
said a monkey. "But it will be fun to try."

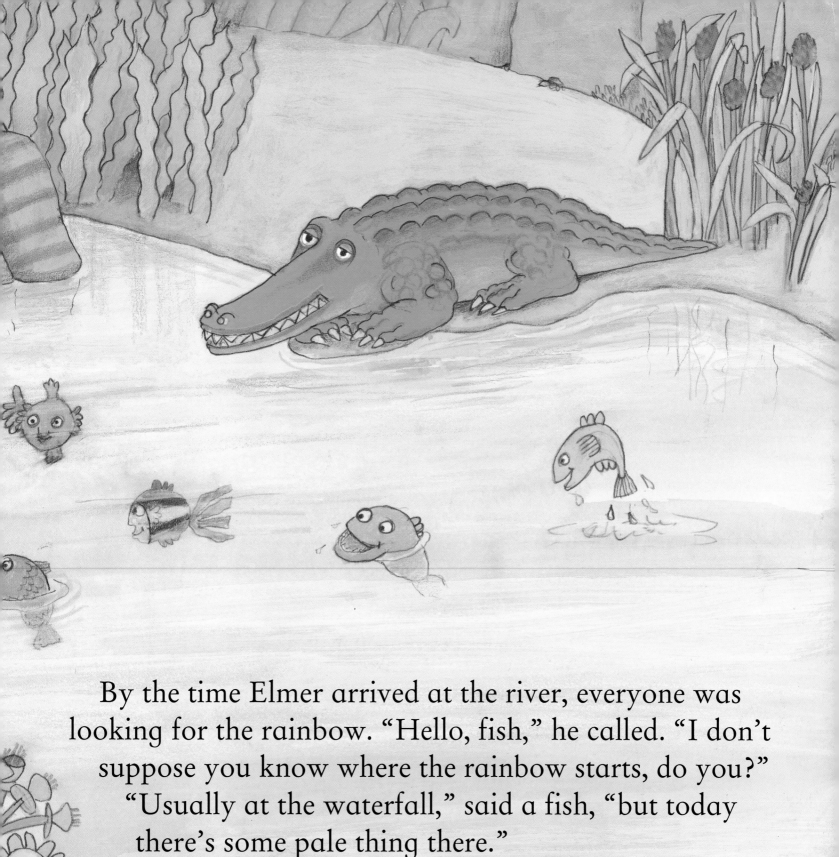

By the time Elmer arrived at the river, everyone was
looking for the rainbow. "Hello, fish," he called. "I don't
suppose you know where the rainbow starts, do you?"
"Usually at the waterfall," said a fish, "but today
there's some pale thing there."
"That's the rainbow!" said Elmer. "Come on, to
the waterfall!"

Sure enough, a colorless rainbow
was coming from the waterfall. The search
was over! Elmer, the fish, and the crocodiles called
loudly to the other animals. Then, without waiting,
Elmer went behind the waterfall.

By the time the other animals arrived, Elmer
was out of sight. Colors gradually began to
appear in the rainbow.
"Hurrah!" cheered the animals.
"But what about Elmer?" whispered an
elephant.

As if in answer, Elmer appeared from behind the waterfall.
He still had his colors! The animals cheered again.
"But Elmer," said an elephant, "you gave your colors to
the rainbow. How can you still have them?"
Elmer chuckled, "Some things you can give and give and
not lose any. Things like happiness or love or my colors."

On the way home, Tiger said, "I wondered
if the rainbow would be patchwork."
Elmer grinned.
"Don't even think about it," said Lion. "We have
enough trouble with a patchwork elephant!"
This time, Elmer laughed out loud.

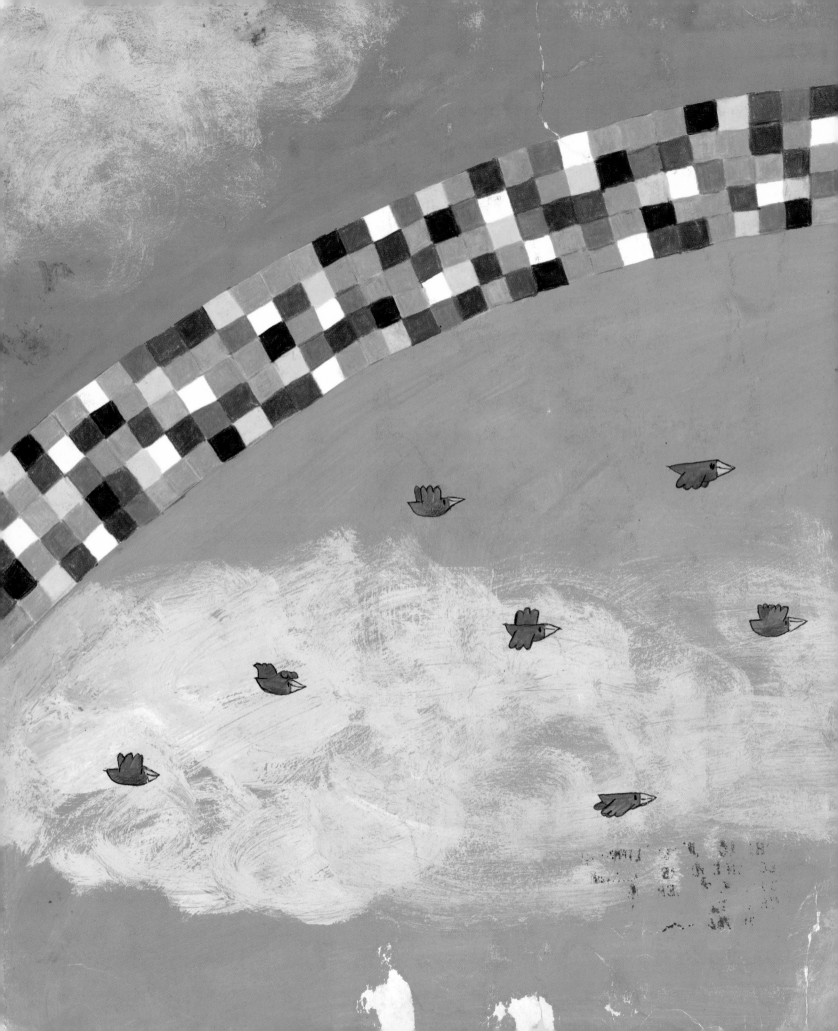